W9-AUN-792

be brave little one

Written and illustrated by
Marianne Richmond

sourcebooks jabberwocky

Published by Sourcebooks Jabberwocky, an imprint of Sourcebooks, Inc.
P.O. Box 4410, Naperville, Illinois 60567-4410
(630) 961-3900
Fax: (630) 961-2168
sourcebooks.com

Library of Congress Cataloging-in-Publication Data is on file with the publisher.

Source of Production: Leo Paper, Heshan City, Guangdong Province China
Date of Production: June 2017
Run Number: 5009460

Printed and bound in China.

LEO 10 9 8 7 6 5 4 3 2 1

Dedicated to
me and to you.

When I look at you,
shining bright as the sun,
I wish for you this...

B

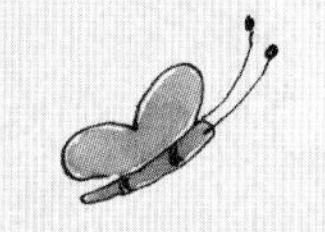

be
brave
little
one!

Be brave to begin
to listen inside
to the voice of your heart,
so truthful and wise.

How far
will I go?
What things
can I be?
PLACES TO SEE
OTIS

When I get to choose
what brave is to me.

Be brave to step up
and try something new.

Be brave to step out
when it isn't for you.

Be brave
to stand up
and tell what
you know.

Be brave
to sit down
and say
a "hello."

Be brave to explore
in the daring unknown.

Be brave to return
to the cozy of home.

Be brave
to be scared,

to stomp
and to cry.

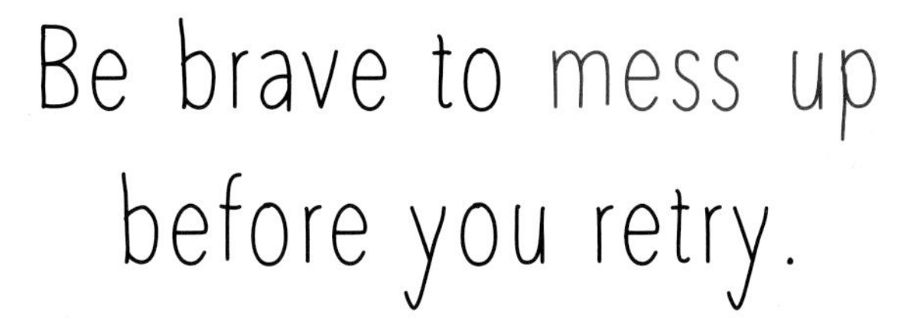

Be brave to mess up
before you retry.

Be brave to believe
in what you can't see—
with the ups and the downs
that are all meant to be.

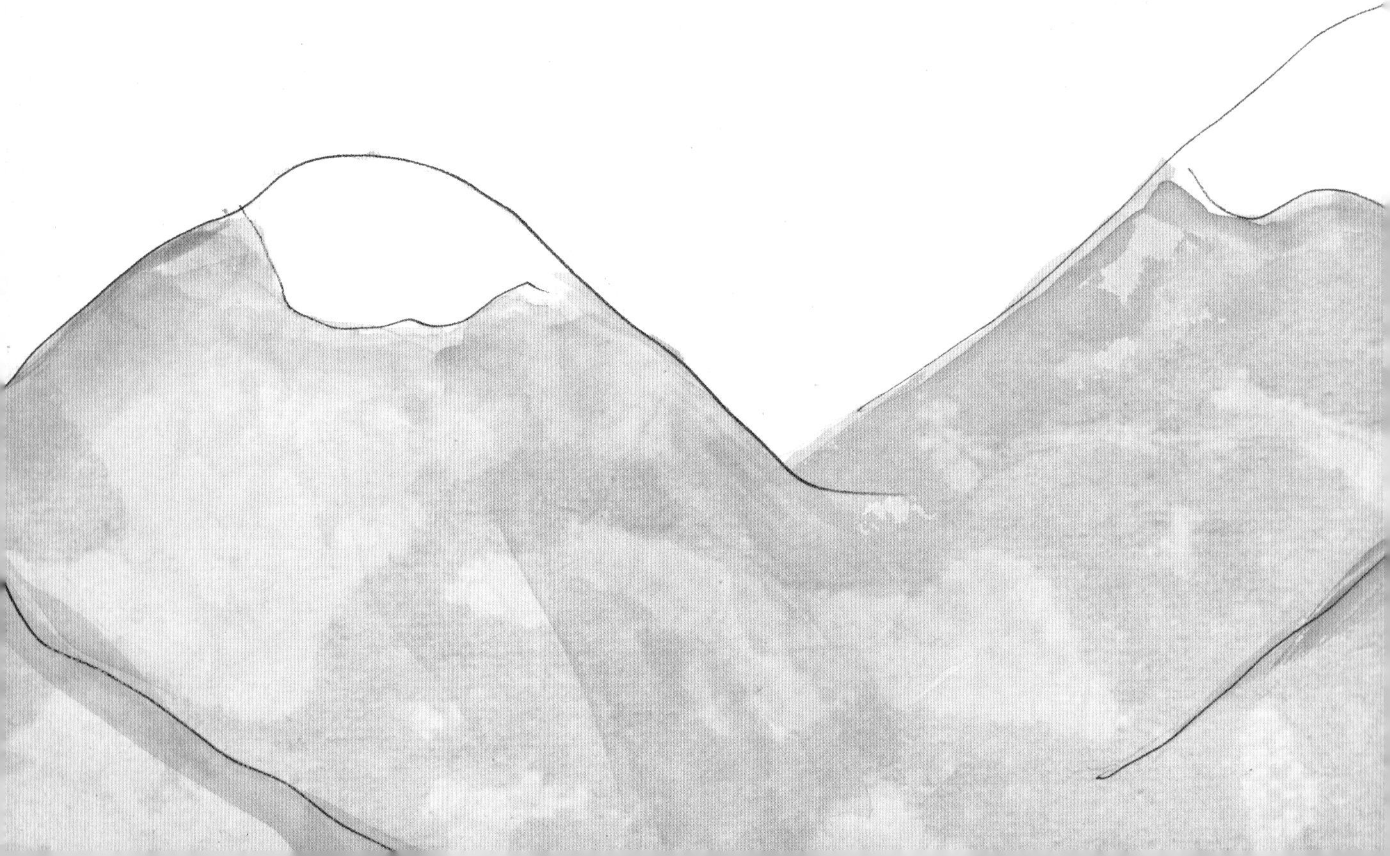

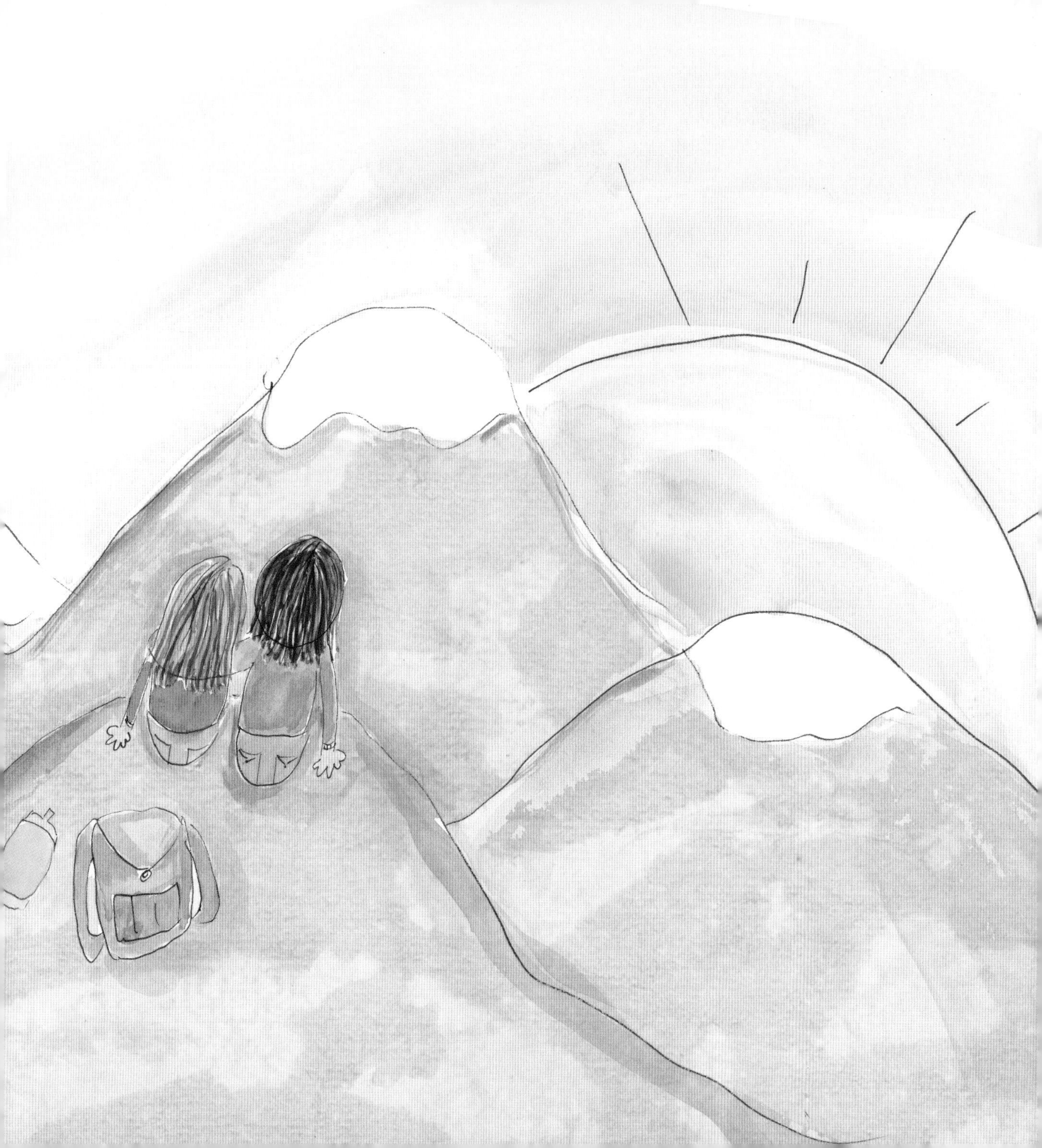

Be brave to keep going
when going is tough.

Be brave to be still
when you've had enough.

Be brave to be with your feelings, each one:

the happy and sad, the silly and glum.

Be brave
to be quiet.

Be brave
to be loud.

Be brave to achieve and be fully proud.

Be brave to BE YOU
on your journey begun.
Let your heart lead the way...

be
brave
little
one!

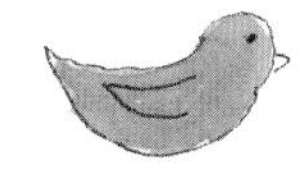

ABOUT THE AUTHOR

Beloved author
and illustrator
Marianne Richmond
has touched the lives
of millions for two
decades through her
heartfelt books and gifts
that help people feel their
feelings and connect with
whom they love.